SAY MERRY CHRISTMAS, Boss

TAYLOR WILSON-WEST

Paperback ISBN: 979-8-9883969-4-9

eBook ISBN: 979-8-9883969-5-6

Cover Design by Indie Editorial, LLC

Illustrations by Roze Stojovska

Edited by Trinity McIntosh, Type A Tweaks

Proofread by Ashley DePointe

Formatting by Taylor Wilson-West

SAY MERRY CHRISTMAS, Boss

To my readers, may your orgasms be plentiful this holiday season.

**partners/vibrators sold seperately*

Author's Note

This is a romantic comedy with **A LOT of spice***. These main characters don't take themselves seriously, so please don't take anything they say or do too seriously, except the romance, they are very much going to be in love.

What to expect going into this read...

- Workplace romance

- Christmas puns

- Powerplay

- Sexually explicit scenes

- Dominant/Submissive

- Dirty talk

*The reason we're all here in the first place, really. Let's not lie to ourselves.

Please enjoy this short spin off novella, I was feeling passionate, and horny and so I told my editor that I did "a thing" and then shoved this in her face and she said it was good so I published it.

You're all welcome.

Eli

The Call...

The little gray bubbles popped up on my screen and disappeared. My stomach turned, I knew this was a bad idea. Ronnie didn't owe me anything, but knowing the type of person she was, I figured....

Relief swept through my system. At least she answered.

I laughed to myself, seeing her name light up my phone screen. I had a sneaking suspicion she would react this way.

Answering her immediate phone call, "It was about a year ago, around Christmas." I told her.

Eli

Mingle Bells

"Mingle Bells, Mingle Bells, Mingle all the way...
I forgot how much I hate these functions to this
day, hey!"

The Barn was nothing like any of the barns
I had seen while in South Carolina this past
winter. This "barn" had unblemished white
walls made of vinyl that tried its best to look
like wood. Perfectly cut beams held up the
structure on the inside. They were decorated
with Edison bulb string lights dangling from
corner to corner, and they even had wooden
wine barrels placed throughout the space.
Everything was too perfect, and far too

polished to be classified as a 'barn'.

I chuckled a little to myself, the southern charm of South Carolina's French Quarter really rubbed off on me while my brother married the woman of his dreams.

Back home in California, I missed them. Garrett and Stacey had made the decision to move not long after they got married. I was nothing but happy for them, but since I still had my apartment leased for the next year, I decided to stay. Why forfeit the money I had already sunk into it?

Christmas music drifted around everyone here in soft notes. Green garland had been wrapped around any and every exposed beam that could house it, red and silver ornaments dotted the evergreens, and I felt myself getting dizzy from the way my eyes bounced every-which-way.

"Let's eat, say hi to your boss, and go." A man's attempted whisper hit my ears from behind me. I swiveled my head that way, he was speaking to Carol from accounting, must be her husband.

Same buddy.

I may be a charismatic guy, but I loathed having to interact with so many people at once.

I had no intention of going tonight. I hadn't been into the office in a few years anyway, so they wouldn't miss me. That was supposed to be the benefit of working remotely, no forced social interaction under the guise of a 'holiday party'. I thought I was off the hook, until my lovely assistant, Ash, told me it would be a good idea if I went. She had done everything she could over the course of the last few weeks to get me to dust off my best suit and show up.

So, I did.

Ash had become one of the most important people in my career, and I hadn't even met her yet... face to face, that was.

She was a virtual assistant, someone heard and not seen. It wasn't that I didn't *want* to see her, it just didn't make a difference. We had no need to video conference when an email was all that was needed in order to communicate effectively.

We both understood it. Honestly, I thought she preferred it. Not once had she asked me what I looked like, or how old I was, nothing. She just did her job, and she did it fantastically.

"Look who decided to show up!" A definitely feminine voice said from behind where I stood.

Turning to get a look at her, she smiled and I opened my arms. Becks had been my boss and mentor for almost twelve years. I started not long after she developed her non-profit. Then, as a lowly summer intern while she toiled away at her dream. Now though, I was her chief financial officer.

Spending those college summers at home wasn't a bad start to climbing up the corporate ladder.

Take that, Garrett.

"Ash said you probably wouldn't come." Becks said, her silver hair was curled and slicked back at her ears. Always a classy lady.

"She bullied me into coming," I gruffed. "Told me, and I quote, *'you owe Becks everything, the LEAST you can do is show your face and say hello, you big hermit.'"*

She laughed and I smiled. There wasn't much I wouldn't do for Becks. The woman who took me under her wing and helped shape me into the man I was today.

"You look like you walked through a glitter factory, Becks." I said, bending down and placing a kiss on her russet cheek.

"It's Christmas, you peacock." She said the nickname I earned years ago with such love I couldn't help the cheeky grin that pulled my lips upward. "I see you dressed for the occasion."

It was true, I pulled my crimson jacket and pants from the back of my closet and paired it with my black leather shoes. I even ironed a white button down for this shindig, and wore a tie. It had been a while since I had put on a suit. With the exception of Garrett's wedding, I didn't think I'd put one on at all this year.

Wild.

I still remember when I was interning, how every man in the building for M&W Enterprises dressed in their best every day. That all changed when Becks decided she didn't want a skyscraper with giant windows to be our home base.

So, everyone who wanted to work from home could, and those that didn't, had an office in an old hotel she had bought and renovated. Becks was the best person I had the pleasure of knowing, and I was honored to call her a genuine friend.

"Mingle, dear." She said, as she lightly patted my arm with her hand in a gesture that meant she would be busy for a while.

She turned, greeting more guests who had walked in the door, and once again I was on my own. Winter here wasn't that cold. Mild I'd say, and in this full outfit I was already starting to sweat, reminding me why I hated suits. People trickled in, all M&W employee's and family. This party was *something else.* I had almost forgotten how over the top Becks tended to make these parties. Especially after she made the decision to go mostly remote, it was her way of keeping her employees and their families close, in spite of the distance.

Becks even had a Santa brought in. Complete with elves with pointy ears, a sleigh, and gifts. Which Santa was giving out to guests like candy. Children squealed and tittered as they unwrapped their toys, and the joy on their faces must've been the reason Becks went to all this trouble. It was adorable, and I had no doubt Becks picked out, and wrapped, every gift herself.

The bar was located on the other side of the room from Santa, and he looked a little too rosy to me. If I was hot, I couldn't imagine how hot he was sitting there, fully Santa suited up, under spotlights to take pictures with children.

I walked toward the elf with the camera, slowly so I wouldn't startle her. She wore bright green tights under a red sweater that had tinsel wrapped around it. When she moved bells jingled, and after she had snapped a few pictures I tapped her lightly on the shoulder.

"Do you know if Santa has any water?" I asked.

Her chestnut hair was thick and wavy down her back, when she swung her head around to see who was speaking, the tendrils of it brushed my arm. I couldn't feel it through the jacket I had on, but when her gray-blue eyes connected with mine all of my hair stood on end.

It was an unfamiliar feeling, like... I knew her.

"Uhm," she said. "I'm not sure." She tucked a lighter strand of hair behind her ear and looked back at the big man in the chair. "But, I could ask?"

"Do I know you?" I asked, puzzled at the notion of possibly knowing this woman.

Her eyes were heavily glittered, and her dark golden cheeks were painted pink, even still. I felt like I *knew* her.

"I don't think so," she said, eyes searching my face. Her lips were glossy and pink, her teeth dug into them as she looked at me.

I didn't know what else to say. Honestly, I'd forgotten what it was I had even come over here for. She was beautiful, and I couldn't think straight. I wouldn't be able to do anything else until I figured out who she was.

"Do you want me to ask him?" She asked, pulling me from my tunnel of thoughts.

"What?"

"Santa, you asked if he had water." Her head tilted to the side as she looked up at me, eyes slightly squinched.

"Oh, right. Yeah, I'll just get him a bottle." I turned and walked away from her, kicking myself for acting like a jackass. God, she probably thought I was an idiot.

Eli

Rockin' Around the Christmas Elf

"Rockin' around the Christmas Elf
At the Christmas party barn
Mistletoe hung where you can see
Every couple tries to stop me."

At the bar I asked for two bottles of water, and a beer. I wasn't sure I could get through another conversation without one. I couldn't get the nagging feeling in my chest to go away.

The bartender handed the ice cold bottles to me and a glass frosted and filled with golden liquid. I took a few gulps, suds clung to my beard and I wiped them away with one of the little red square napkins on the wooden bar top.

With that sampling of liquid courage, I made my way through the now crowded space back toward Santa and the elf. I offered the bottles to her and she took them, quickly bringing them to Santa before another child could clamor up his leg into his lap. Poor man needed a break.

I couldn't imagine smiling like he was for the entirety of this event, even if it was only a few hours.

He nodded his thanks in my direction when the short elf woman pointed to me, and I took that as my cue to walk away. I wasn't going to figure out how I knew her by stalking her all night.

I needed to give up on the notion of figuring it out and *mingle*, as Becks so kindly suggested.

"Aye, Peacock," Jeremiah's deep voice broke through my thoughts, and I smiled.

"It's been a long time," I said, wrapping his hand with mine and pulling him in. We pated shoulders in the typical 'bro hug' and stepped back.

"Look at this mop!" He twisted his hand on top of my head, mussing the curls I'd just styled not long ago.

"Yeah, Becks keeps me too busy to get a haircut."

"I'll bet." He nodded and smiled, as another man we knew entered The Barn, "I'm gonna get a beer, want a refill?"

"Nah man, I'm good." I declined politely, better to only have one, I didn't want to stay longer than I had to. It was a good evening for a quick jog, and a long soak.

Microphone static and feedback jarred everyone from their conversations, and eyes swiveled toward the makeshift stage near where Santa was perched.

Becks held a glass of champagne and chuckled into the mic, "That'll get your attention!"

Everyone laughed with her, she had that essence about her. The kind that made you feel like you were one of the most important people on the planet. The elf clad woman I couldn't stop thinking about, joined her on stage, holding a shiny plaque award. She was glowing under the stage lights, absolutely beautiful.

"I won't babble on, I promise," Becks started her speech, as if she could ever be considered a babbler. "Tonight is about celebration, and you all deserve it. But there's one of you that I'd be remiss if I didn't personally thank, and thoroughly embarrass at the same time."

I loved it when Becks did her surprise awards.

They were always hilarious, and I couldn't wait to see which poor soul would be roasted.

"Many of you already know him, I mean, he's pretty hard to miss." Everyone laughed, "When he first toddled into my office, solemn faced and in an ill fitted suit, I knew he would either be a dud, or an incredible asset to our cause."

People started looking around, giving each other eyebrow wiggles and smirks.

"He's come a long way since he started," she continued. "We've watched him grow from a sulking teen into a... slightly less-sulking man."

The beer in my stomach sloshed around, she wouldn't... "We have watched him flounder with countless women, struggle through college, and then graduate with honors. We watched him grow taller in the years he's been employed with us, and I am honored to award our very own Peacock, the award for..."

I couldn't process the words after she said my nickname. *I* was the poor bastard who was just roasted. *Mother-fuck.*

Jeremiah clapped me on the back, laughter flushed his face as he pushed me toward the stage. I must have blacked out, because I didn't remember approaching the stage, climbing the steps, and coming face to face with the stunning elf woman again.

Her curves were on full display as she smiled and handed me the placard that I didn't bother to read. My eyes were locked on her.

Becks was still talking, letting everyone know the time and how much longer there was left. She told everyone to enjoy the free booze and food, but I couldn't focus.

My ears were fuzzy. The beauty before me started to speak, but I couldn't hear her over the buzzing in my head. The lights on the stage were hot, sweat slicked down my spine.

I smiled at her because I didn't know what else to do.

Becks turned and ushered us behind Santa's sled.

"Finally!" She said, waving her hands between us, "I've been waiting for what feels like years to introduce you two."

The elf woman dipped her head and I saw a blush creep across her cheeks.

"Eli, this is Ashtrid, my granddaughter." When I didn't respond, Becks offered, "Your assistant."

Double mother-fuck.

"Everyone calls me Ash," she looked up at me through her lashes.

"Hi." I managed to get out. Then, because I hadn't been embarrassed enough, I waved like a total dweeb.

She laughed, a nervous lilt, or maybe I was projecting my thoughts onto her. If I had known she was this beautiful, I would have definitely asked to have video chats.

Wait, is that against policy? I was so going to get fired for sexual harassment.

"I'm gonna go finish up with Santa," she said to Becks, "Nice to finally meet you in person, Boss."

My dick twitched behind my slacks with her use of my title passing those bow-shaped lips.

"Fire me," I swiveled to Becks. "Fire me, right fucking now."

She laughed and laid a hand on my arm, "She's something, isn't she."

"Becks, you tell me right now to go pack my shit."

"Eli," she began, "That isn't necessary, I wouldn't trust her with anyone else."

"Then I quit."

I started to walk away, but her hand on my arm squeezed, "I don't accept."

"Like hell, Becks." I'd plead with her right now if I had to, "I can't explain it..."

"I'm not asking you to," she smirked. "There was a certain sparkle in her eye when she saw your picture not long ago, and when I found out how well you two worked together, I thought, maybe you all could be... more."

"Becks, this isn't the eighteen hundreds, since when do you play matchmaker? I don't want to settle down, you know this. It's not that others haven't tried to get me to commit, it's just not something I want," I tried to warn her, and remind myself.

"I have a feeling, for the right one, you will." Becks walked away and threw over her shoulder, "I expect you in the office Monday morning, bright and early, Peacock."

Ash

Santa Maybe

"Santa maybe, just slip a dick right under the
tree for me
Been an awful good girl
Santa maybe, so hurry down my pussy tonight."

He was even more handsome in real life than in his pictures. Cheese and crackers, he was stunning, super-model worthy. What was he doing being a chief financial officer?

No way that man went to college and became a boring office man. Especially not the one who I had been working with for the past couple of months.

I couldn't wrap my brain around it. Even as I snapped pictures of the little ones on Santa's lap for my grandmother's party, I couldn't stop thinking about Eli.

I kept sneaking glances over to where he and my grandmother were still talking. He looked upset, and she looked like the cat that got the canary. Leave it to my grandmother to be plotting...

Stopping myself from wondering what he really thought of me, I threw myself into the elf persona, and the kids loved it. Even though I didn't want any of my own anytime soon, I enjoyed their little awed faces and giggles.

When Santa finally called it quits I circled the room, speaking to the people I recognized and introducing myself to the ones I didn't. I was a people person, through and through.

It didn't matter to me that I was dressed like an elf, with a pound of glitter on my face. I was having so much fun, and I couldn't contain my holiday excitement.

Even if it was still two weeks away.

Christmas has always been a holiday I enjoyed, not because of the presents, or the fun holiday outings, but the food and family gatherings that always took place.

I had the biggest family, and my grandmother Becks was the glue that held us all together. She made sure all of us cousins got along and appreciated each other. I also had three brothers and two sisters, we were all thick as thieves.

Trying not to look for Eli across the room was difficult. My eyes kept gravitating toward him, as if my instincts were tuned into his orbit.

He quickly looked away every time our eyes would connect, which should have been my sign to leave him be. I just... couldn't.

Becks found me then, "Having a fancy, huh?"

I looked back at her where she had stopped behind me and rolled my eyes. Of course I was looking my fill, he was handsome.

"Let's walk, shall we?"

It wasn't really a question. Becks led me around like a prized bird, telling everyone who would listen–which was everyone–about how I was making my way through the company. It was touching how proud she was, but there was really only one person I wanted to talk to.

Eli's tall frame came into view, and I took a deep breath.

"Star of the show tonight, Peacock?" Becks said, prompting him to spin around. God, he smelled so good, like mint and bourbon.

"All thanks to you, Becks."

He didn't sound very amused, which seemed to make my grandmother all the more happy. The creases at her eyes became deeper with her smile, and she patted my elbow giving me a clear signal that I was supposed to take over the conversation.

Well, here goes...

"It's so nice to finally talk to you in person, Eli." I started, easy, no jumbled words, no word vomit, just formal.

His brows lifted, a small movement I wouldn't have noticed if I weren't paying attention.

"You as well, Ash." He was stiff, much stiffer than when he'd asked if Santa needed a drink. Did I smell? Shit, did I forget to put deodorant on?

"I'll leave you kids to it, then." Grandmother said before flitting off in the opposite direction.

We were both silent, what else could I say? I didn't want to embarrass myself, not anymore than my outfit was right now.

"This isn't my usual outfit," I offered, pulling up one side of my dress to make the little bells jingle.

"I'd hope not."

His eyes widened as if he didn't expect to say that out loud. I laughed, I couldn't help it. He was either disgusted with my outfit, or thoroughly embarrassed by his blunder. Either way it made me laugh.

Eli 

Baby Please Cum Home

"Oh, oh
Yeah, yeah oh oh
Ooh yeah
the cum's comin' down
(Ashhtrid) I'm watchin' it fall
(Ashtrid) It's just us around
(Ashtrid) baby, please cum more"

Her fucking laugh.

It was… alluring, in the best way. Like she was a damn siren calling me out to sea and I think I would happily drown.

"I'm sorry," I began, "I didn't mean to be rude."

She snorted and doubled over, waving her hands in front of her face.

"No, no," she hiccuped, "I get it."

"You do?" Was I *that* obvious?

"You don't like Christmas very much, do you?" She laughed into the back of her hand when she finally stepped closer.

"It's not that," I hesitated, because it *was* that, "Okay, I don't hate the holidays."

"But you don't like them, either?" She prompted.

I couldn't argue with her, I just didn't really have anyone to celebrate with anymore, since Garrett moved away, and our parents lived on a different continent.

I shrugged, "I don't really see the point."

"The point in celebrating?" She asked, voice raising an octave.

"All of it, I guess."

I wanted out of this conversation, I was bound to make a bigger mess of it, and then what? She would go running back to Becks informing her of my ineptitude at conversation. I ran a hand down my face, rubbing at my neatly trimmed stubble. I was in way over my head.

"Do you," Ash's voice pulled me from my thoughts, "Maybe want to get out of here?"

"With you?" I asked, surprise must have been written on my face, because she giggled.

"Yes, with me."

I nodded, because I was suddenly too hot in this place, and I desperately wanted her alone.

"Let me grab my bag," she put her hand on my elbow and I swear a spark lit up my insides, "Meet me at the entrance in five?"

"Y-yeah," I stuttered and cleared my throat, "Yeah, sure."

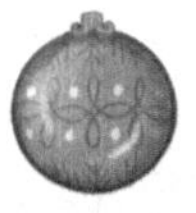

She had a bag slung over her shoulder and a grin on her face when she finally found me standing outside.

"Did you drive?" She asked, pointing to the sparse parking lot.

"I did, yes."

"Well, Boss, which one's yours?" She started toward the few cars in the lot, most people walked from the office building, or took a car here.

I twirled my key ring round my finger and nodded toward my baby. She looked back at me with a wink when she spotted my cherry red '67 Chevelle.

"Nice car, *Peacock*," she enunciated my nickname, teasing me.

"Thanks," I said, "Are you really going to get into a practical strangers car?"

"You're my boss, I doubt you'd try to murder me. But sure, let's play that scenario out." Her blue eyes rolled, and I wanted to swat her ass for it, "Are you going to kill me, Boss?"

"You might be the one killing me," I joked half-heartedly.

She laughed and threw open the passenger door once I clicked the locks, "I want to show you something."

"I'm driving," I scoffed, "Wouldn't I be the one showing you something?"

She held her hands out, "Then I'll drive."

"Uh, no. I don't think so, Little Elf."

"Okay then, think you can follow my directions?"

It wasn't a far drive. The diner she brought us to was lit up in all kinds of Christmas lights, from multi-colored to white bulbs, all the way to candy canes lining the walkway.

"Festive," I mocked.

She ran her hands over the candy canes as we walked into the diner. The inside was worse, I counted three Christmas trees total, ornaments hung from every possible nook and cranny, it was like the North Pole threw up in here.

Children ran around the tables, some clothed in nice polos, others in Christmas themed PJ sets. Some even had hand-me-down clothes on.

"What?" I had to turn sideways to avoid being run over by three children chasing each other.

"Ashtrid!" A slender woman in a Santa hat hollered.

"Lindsay!" She yelled back and grabbed my hand, pulling me toward the back of the diner, where a row of silver catering looking dishes waited. Half of them were almost gone, and people rotated through the kitchen doors with new ones.

"You brought extra hands?" Lindsay asked, nodding in my direction.

"I did!"

"Uh, wha–" I began, but Ash pulled me into the kitchen and placed a red striped apron over my neck.

"All you have to do is scoop food onto plates," she secured the ties around my waist and placed her hands on her ample hips, "Think you can handle that?"

"What?" I couldn't form a complete sentence

before she pushed me out the door and placed me behind the stuffing.

"Scoop, and smile, Boss," She said, standing beside me at the gravy tray.

I leaned over to her, "I have no idea what just happened in the last ten minutes, care to fill me in?"

She laughed and said, "I thought you could use a little holiday cheer."

"This is holiday cheer?"

She nodded, "Just wait."

Families came through the line with timid smiles and grateful 'thank you's', and I started to piece together what Ash meant. This was a meal drive, of sorts. But some of these people didn't look homeless, and I didn't see anyone accepting any money. So it had to be some sort of charity work for low income families or those struggling financially to afford food for the holidays.

After replenishing my tray twice, the line seemed to die down a bit. My feet hurt, but the smile on my face was real. I couldn't remember the last time I'd smiled and meant it. These people were so excited to have a warm meal, and for their children to have full bellies.

"I volunteer here with Lindsay twice a month, sometimes more if we can get the food," Ash told me as we cleaned up the serving line.

"It's that busy?"

She turned her head to look at me, it felt like the first time, and I felt my chest cave in a little at her beauty.

"It was Becks idea," Ash started, and I should have known, "She loves feeding people, and I love seeing families not have to struggle to put food in their children's bellies."

"You can't be real," I blurted. God, what was it

about her that made my brain forget its filter?

She laughed, "I am, but I could argue the same thing."

My eyes snapped to hers, "What do you mean?"

"Come on, Boss," she scoffed. "Look at you."

Lindsay took the small moment of silence in our conversation, and offered us both plates and a table in the back part of the diner. It wasn't exactly quiet, but it wasn't overrun with noise and children either.

"What did you mean, 'look at you'?" I asked her, just as she took a bite of turkey.

She dropped the plastic fork and chewed faster.

"Seriously?" She asked after swallowing her food.

I nodded.

"You're," she paused, waving her hand around

my face, "Gorgeous."

I felt my cheeks flush with pride, and straightened my spine.

"There's the peacock my grandmother talks about."

And, deflated.

She laughed, "It's not a bad thing!"

"You think I'm gorgeous?" I asked, because I couldn't tell if she meant it as a passing compliment or if she was crushing on me as much as I was crushing on her.

She bit her bottom lip and nodded.

"I think you're the most beautiful woman I've ever seen in my life." I reached across the table and gripped her chin, using my thumb to brush her bottom lip. If I was going to take a chance, it would be now, and I wasn't going to let the chance to get to know her better pass me by.

Her eyes went wide, and she smiled a big

goofy smile that made my lips quirk up.

"Do you want to come back to my place with me?"

She nodded and sprang up from the booth, grabbing my hand, she yelled a goodbye to Lindsay and then we were in my car.

Ash

I Want an Orgasm for Christmas

"I want an orgasm for Christmas
Only an orgasm will do
I don't want a raise, no sticky-icky fuckboy
I want a man to play with and enjoy."

His mouth crashed into mine as he backed me up against the wall in his apartment. My ass hit the wall hard and the picture beside it fell with a crash and clang. He didn't stop, so I didn't think he cared.

Hands, his hands were everywhere, roaming over my curves and full breasts. He squeezed and kneaded my love handles, groaning into my mouth.

"Fuck, you're so sexy," he said between kissing my lips and neck.

His hard body pressed into my soft one, and I felt my pussy clench and drip with arousal. He hooked his thumbs into the hem of my shirt and pushed up, exposing my new Christmas bra. The pattern was so fun and funky, I couldn't help buying it.

He chuckled and ran a finger over the swell of my tits, following the trail his finger left with his mouth. I had to sink my teeth into my lower lip to keep from groaning at the contact.

"Give me all your noises, Little Elf," he whispered, as if he knew I was holding back. "I want to hear what you sound like when I make you cum."

Shivers ran up my body, causing my skin to pebble.

I whimpered into his kiss as he undid his belt. The metallic click was like a sugar rush to my clit. Rubbing my legs together I pulled my shirt off completely, exposing all of the stretch marks and cellulite that marked my body.

Some people had given me shit about these things, but honestly, I loved my body. Every single dent and dimple, it's what made me, *me*. I had always been a mid size girl, and I wouldn't trade my map of curves and valleys for all the diet pills in the world.

His eyes darkened taking in my body, as I went to unhook my festive bra, his gaze lasered in on my hands.

"Don't," he grabbed my wrists and pulled them back to the front, "That's my job."

His fingers made nimble work of the clasps, and my breasts tumbled free. His intake of breath had *me* acting like a peacock and pushing my tits toward him, begging to be touched.

My knees felt weak, like jelly, and we hadn't even gotten to the good stuff. I went to my knees before him, and he backed up.

"Wha..." I started.

"Shhhh, let me look at you," his voice soothed my nerves, "You look so fucking sweet on your knees for me."

I blushed from my hairline to my toes.

He took slow steps backward, his eyes never leaving mine, and sat down on the plush couch. His legs splayed wide, hands on his knees. He was so fucking hot, I thought I might die if he didn't let me do something, anything to alleviate the tension.

"I'm going to tell you exactly what I want," he licked his lips. "Think you can keep up?"

I nodded eagerly, waiting for him to

command me. I wanted to be used, and God I wanted him to make me feel... otherworldly.

"Take off those tights," he commanded, and I did. Slowly I stripped them off my hips, sliding them down my thighs and standing to pull them completely off, one foot at a time. He sat back, his erection straining against his crimson slacks.

"Good girl, back on your knees for me, Little Elf," he crooned.

I rolled my eyes, and took a deep breath as I slowly lowered to my knees, he was checking all the boxes and we had barely started.

"Now, crawl to me."

I sucked in a breath and crawled, making sure to exaggerate my hip movements. Lengthening my legs and stretching my arms out. He groaned in approval and rubbed his hand over his cock.

"Beg, my little whore," he smirked when I got close enough to place my hands on his knees. I sat back on my bare feet and did as he asked.

"I want to taste you, Boss." I whimpered out, God, I was so ready to have him in my mouth. "Please," I added.

He unbuttoned his pants, and agonizingly slowly moved the zipper down. His eyes drilled into my head, I could feel the heat of his stare without looking.

"No. I think you can do better."

I snapped my face up to his.

"Please? Please, Boss, I want to feel your cock in my mouth. I need to taste your cum on my tongue." I pleaded, I was so horny, and I wanted to make him feel good.

He cupped my chin with his other hand and ran his thumb over my lips. I licked his calloused finger and he chuckled.

"Eagerness suits you."

"*Please*, Boss."

He pulled himself from his boxers, and my *stars* I think it was the prettiest fucking dick I had ever seen. Smooth skin with veins that ran up his sizable length, to a perfectly rounded tip that had a shiny dollop of precum just waiting for me to lick.

I wanted to know what he tasted like, he smelled incredible. Like sin, desires, and spice.

His fingers gripped my chin and tipped my face up, making my eyes flutter to his.

"Make it sloppy, Little Elf," he leaned down to ghost his mouth against mine, "I want everything you've got to give."

His hand moved to the back of my head and he shoved my mouth down around his cock without warning. I felt a rush of arousal pool in my Christmas thong, as the tip of his perfect length hit the back of my throat. I moaned around him, eyes shutting at the feeling of being so *handled*.

Spit pooled around the base of him as he held me there, waiting for me to gag or give up. I wouldn't do either, instead I made a noise of approval and relaxed my throat. He groaned at my admission of him and released my head so I could gulp down air. Stringy spit connected us and it was arguably the sexiest thing I'd ever seen. Nice and messy, just like he wanted.

I licked him from balls to tip, using my hands to rub and squeeze the smooth skin of his sack. He groaned and his head fell back against the couch. I returned to his cock and bobbed, hollowing out my cheeks and sucking, the sounds I made were new to me, but in the most erotic way possible.

His hand threaded through my hair as I used

my spit to work his balls while I used my mouth to tease the tip of his cock.

"Touch yourself while you enjoy my cock, you filthy fucking whore," our eyes connected at his words and I did as he asked, using the hand I'd had wrapped around the base of him to run through my cunt. I was so fucking wet.

Sucking sounds came from my panties as I worked my clit and fucked my fingers. I was so horny I felt like I could combust right there, on the floor between his legs.

"Listen to the sounds your body makes for me," he smoothed my hair before shoving my head down again. "I can't wait to slide my fucking cock into your wet pussy."

"Mmmmmm," I cried as I built my orgasm higher.

"Cum on your fingers, baby," he whispered, still holding my head where he wanted me as he thrust his cock in and out of my throat. "Show me how fucking hot you find this."

I shoved two fingers inside of my dripping pussy, and grinded my hips against the heel of my hand. His cock hit the back of my throat deliciously and I fucking lost it. I cried out while he continued his thrusts, working myself over and feeling the rush of my orgasm flood my body.

"I'm going to cum down your throat for being such an eager little slut," he warned, and God I wanted nothing more as I rocked on my fingers to wrench the last of my orgasm free.

He stilled as he came deep down my throat, both hands tangled in my hair. When he was done twitching he lifted me up and reached down to pull me onto his lap.

"Holy Hannah, you're stronger than you look."

He laughed against my neck and praised me, "You did such a fucking good job, Little Elf."

I cuddled into his chest, letting my thighs cage him in.

"I'm not done with you yet." He warned, noting my fluttering eyes, "I plan on seeing just how many of those I can get from you tonight."

Hell. Fucking. Yes.

Eli

You'll be Fucked for Christmas

"You'll be fucked for Christmas
You can plan on me
Please take my cum and orgasms
And strangle my dick for me."

She listened beautifully, a good little filthy elf.

I let her rest for a beat. I hadn't lied to her when

I said I wanted to see just how many orgasms

I could give her. She responded so well to my

words.

I was growing hard again thinking about it.

I ran my hand over her back, she was a big

woman, and I couldn't get enough of her. Some

part of my brain knew I should slow down. That we needed to talk about a few things first, like, did she have a safe word? Was she on birth control? Tested for STI's?

Fuck.

Running my hand through my hair I tried not to spiral.

When I looked down she was looking up at me with her icy blue eyes.

"Hi, Boss."

Welp. My lips tipped up, without my permission.

"We need to have a chat about a few things, Little Elf." I stated, and I could hear the cold detachment in my tone.

For what it was worth, she didn't flinch, just moved off my lap and pointed down the hall, "Bathroom?"

"Only door to the left," I nodded in that

direction.

She picked up her bag that she'd dropped during our... lusty haze, and disappeared behind the door, but she didn't close it.

"What do you want to know?" Her voice drifted through the whole apartment like bells, and my jaw hit the floor. This woman, she wasn't real. She was perfect, and she seemed to read my mind.

"How are you so..." I couldn't find the right words.

"Adorable? Irresistible? A fucking goddess?" She supplied.

"Calm?" My brain conjured thoughts of her out every weekend with a poor fella left satisfied but broken hearted. There was no way she was single. "Please, tell me you aren't seeing anyone."

Her laugh bounced around the whole

apartment, "Single as Kris Kringle." She stepped out of the bathroom, still clad in her Christmas lingerie and... fucking Christmas sweater patterned, knee-high stockings. Did she keep extra pairs hidden in her bag? "Well I guess the old man does have a wife, but does anyone ever see her?"

What the hell was she mumbling about? I couldn't focus on anything except her legs. The way she leaned so confidently on my counter, like this wasn't the first time. God help me, I was in way over my head with this woman.

"Are *you* seeing someone?" She asked me, and I froze. I didn't 'see' women, we fucked, they left, and that was that. It didn't require any fan-fair, and I especially didn't *talk* to them. She giggled, pulling me from my thoughts.

"Uh, no." I answered her, "I'm not seeing anyone."

"I figured." She shrugged, and I didn't know if I should feel offended or not. "I mean, this is clearly a bachelor pad."

I looked around, everything was in its place, and I had a few pictures hanging up. What did she mean by that comment?

"Is that a bad thing?"

"No," she stalked back over to where I was still sitting with my cock out, which I promptly tucked away, even though it was still semi-hard.

"I feel like I should know more about you. How long have we been working together, yet I know next to nothing?" I blurted. Wow, that was a great pick up line. Great job, *Boss*.

"I'm twenty-nine and my star sign is leo, which may tell you a bit more about me than you're ready to know. I've been in California for about two years now, I live with my grandmother Becks, you may know her," she winked and continued, "I'm clean as of last week and I have an IUD. So no kiddos for me any time soon."

Wow. Okay, she was... weird. But in a way that made me hunger for more.

"I'm thirty-five, and I have no idea what a star sign is and I don't care to learn. I'm also clean, I get tested every month, and I've lived here for quite a while. I actually used to live with my brother but he's married now, and–" I trailed off not sure if I should say this next part out loud but figured since we were being open and honest, I'd give her my most raw truth, "I'm not sure if I ever want kids."

She plopped down on the couch, placing her legs on top of mine immediately. The gesture surprised me, the casual intimacy of it but in a this-feels-normal, type of way.

"Well, is there anything else you need to know, Boss?"

I couldn't think of anything else, "I guess not."

She laughed, and leaned back over the arm of the couch. Stretching out her stomach and exposing just the barest hint of under boob. I groaned, readjusting myself.

I had plans for us that spanned the entire night, and my over eager dick wasn't going to ruin those.

Ash

Let Us Fuck, Let Us Fuck, Let Us Fuck

"Though the weather outside is mild
And the tension inside is... wild
And since we've no place to hide
Let Us Fuck, Let Us Fuck, Let Us Fuck."

He asked a lot of questions.

I wasn't surprised, I mean I did just pant my horny mess all over him while I gave him the best blow job I had ever given.

He was bound to wonder why I felt so comfortable. This was way out of character for me though, so I wasn't sure how I would answer that question when he eventually asked. All I knew for certain was, I wanted to fuck my boss. And I wanted to do it soon.

He moved his hands up and down my Christmas sweater style stockings, massaging my legs, almost like he didn't realize he was doing it. His eyes were unfocused, brows scrunched up tight, making me wonder what he was thinking. Was this the moment he would realize this was a bad idea and try to send me on my way?

"Do you have something on your mind, Boss?" I asked, growing tired of waiting on him to find the man who fucked my mouth not twenty minutes ago, and come back from wherever his current thoughts were spiraling.

His head swiveled and his eyes locked on mine, I could imagine the way he would wreck my body in the best way. I just needed him to allow himself to do it. The turmoil of his wants and needs were written all over his face, like he was battling with the angel and devil on his shoulders. One telling him this would feel so good, because *we* were so good together. The other saying he'd already gone too far, that I was his employee, that this was *wrong*. I wouldn't try and push him either way.

This was his choice and he had to decide if I was worth it.

"If we do this," he started, and I snorted, we already did 'this', but I pinched my lips and let him continue, "We can't tell anyone."

"Because..." I was failing to see why anyone would care if he fucked me, assistant or not.

"Because you work for me. It would be viewed as a gross misuse of power."

I practically purred, "I'd love for you to show me a gross misuse of power."

He eyed me sharply, as if I wasn't taking this

seriously. Honestly, I knew him better than he thought I did, and I had a feeling he knew me more than he wanted to admit to himself. But like before, I didn't want to point out all the phone calls and emails we'd had.

"I don't want anyone giving you a hard time," he finally stated.

Again, I snorted, but come *on*. He was practically spoon feeding me material.

"I definitely don't mind a hard time," I couldn't help myself. I looked up at him and smiled a cheesy smile.

"Ash," he groaned, clearly fed up with my shit. "I don't know how..."

"You don't commit, you aren't the type," I cut him off, "I know, and I'm okay with it."

"You are?" He said, eyebrows reaching his hairline.

"You might not even be a good fuck anyway,"

I quipped.

The look on his face? God, it was priceless. His eyes darkened in challenge, and his lips parted barely enough to get a breath out before he had me pinned under his body.

He took his time, nothing rushed us as he ran featherlight fingertips over my exposed skin. Causing my skin to pebble and my senses to heighten.

His lips pulled back into a predatory smile, "Your body reacts so well to me."

My eyes rolled back as he brought his mouth down to my bra, he kissed and nipped at the fabric covering my sensitive skin.

His calloused hands roamed over my bare flesh, one trailed up my neck, cupped my chin, and he kissed me, slowly. Savoring.

I teased him with my tongue, hoping to bring out that dominant side again. I was getting so wet just thinking about how much I'd loved being on my knees for him, worshiping his brilliant cock.

In an instant, he seemed to have made his choice as he delved his tongue into my mouth, tangling it with mine. They danced for dominance, claiming each other like this might be the last time. I was a breathless panting mess when he pulled back and peeled down the cups of my bra.

My breasts spilled out, going to either side of my rib cage. My nipples drew up at the sudden temperature change. The skin around them tightening, and my nipples becoming almost painfully hard with anticipation.

"Fuck me, you're stunning." The words must have surprised him, with the way his eyes flared and his mouth popped open.

"I'm trying to," I giggled.

He bit his lip, and growled.

Fuckkkkkkk. That was so hot, way hotter than any man should have a right to be.

He massaged my breasts, kneading them and planting kisses along my ribs. It was a new feeling, I'd never had a man pay that much attention to my body. It was like he wanted to burn my imprint into his mind.

So he would never forget.

I wasn't about to complain, it was empowering and down right sexy as hell. I groaned and pushed my hands into his curls. They were soft and luscious strands, honey blond and dark blond mixed to make the perfect summertime locks.

He made a noise in the back of his throat and shifted his body. His legs bracketed my thighs, and my hands fell to my sides.

"Lift up." He commanded, and I did, placing

my breasts flush with his abdomen. He was still covered with his dress shirt and tie, and the soft fabric rubbed against my nipples.

He made quick work of my bra, unclasping the material and throwing it somewhere behind my head. The heaviness of my breasts caused me to sigh.

His hand circled my throat, thumb under my chin on one side, four fingers firm on the other. He tilted my head up, making my eyes find his.

"I'm going to enjoy wrecking you, Little Elf," he said, and I melted into goo.

Eli

Deck my Balls

"Deck my balls with cum from Ashtrid,
Fu-u-u-u-u-u-u-uck!
' Tis the season to be cuming."

Her pupils dilated, and I smirked. My words affected her, and God did I love her doe grey-blue eyes on me.

Like I was the sun that orbited her sky.

"Are you going to be a good slutty elf and give me what I want?"

I already told her I wanted more orgasms, and if she wasn't ready yet, I would wait. My muscles strung tight as I waited for her to answer. She tried nodding in my grip and I tutted.

"Words, Little Elf." My voice grew deeper as anticipation rose higher.

"Yes," she whispered.

"Yes, what?" I bent down to growl against her cheek.

"Yes, Boss."

I sucked in a long breath, as if drinking in her submission. I kissed her, stroking her tongue with mine.

When she began to squirm, I pushed her back down onto the couch. The cushions cradled her curves with ease as I moved my mouth down her body.

Sucking her perfect tits into my mouth, brushing my teeth along the soft skin there. I took my time, mapping her body with my lips, tongue, and teeth.

I left little marks all over her skin, making my

way down her body as her moans of pleasure drove me wild. When I gripped her thong she sucked in a breath.

"Easy," I whispered against her plump hip.

Her skin smelt like peppermint, tasted like sugar, and I knew one time would never be enough. I was so fucked, in so deep with this woman and I didn't give one single fuck. The material of her thong slipped down her slick thighs, revealing a freshly waxed pussy.

Not a hair in sight.

It glistened and she rubbed her ample thighs together as much as she could with mine between them. I sat back on my heels and groaned at the sight. Tenderly, I placed my hands on the inside of each knee and pushed her thighs apart so that I could get to my prize. If I was going to burn for this, I was going to taste her first. Slowly, I leaned forward and licked the top of her cunt where it just started to separate.

She gasped and bucked her upper body, leaning up on her elbows.

"Watch me, Little Elf. I'm going to devour your pussy like a man starved," I told her, my voice growing husky with every filthy word I said.

Her eyes blew wide and cheeks tinted pink. I smiled a wolfish smile and spread her open with my thumbs. Massaging the backs of her thighs, I feasted on her. Sucked her clit into my mouth and *God* she reacted.

The muscles in her legs tightened with every suck and stroke of my tongue. Her deep moans of pleasure were like sleigh bells to my ears.

I teased her entrance with my tongue, flicking her clit as I made a few passes.

"Cum on my tongue you naughty little elf," I

commanded as I shoved two fingers into her tight pussy. "Show me how much you want my cock instead of my fingers."

She nodded and began rubbing her nipples, plucking and pinching them as she rode my hand. I watched her, dazed by the way her body moved and rolled.

She was utter perfection.

I couldn't wait any longer, dipping my head back down I nipped her clit, and she yelped, followed by a hissed, "Yessss." When her legs locked down, caging my head between her thighs, I sucked harder, tongue circling her clit and pumping my fingers in and out of her.

She was fucking drenched, and I curled my fingers, pushing her into what I hoped would be a spec-fucking-tacular orgasm.

"Break, baby," I whispered against her sensitive flesh. "Shatter for me, and I'll swallow every drop."

And she fucking did.

Her legs clenched my body, as she moaned and shook under my direction. I didn't stop fucking her with my fingers, I wanted to drown in her ecstasy.

The damn broke as she cried out and true to my word, I caught every messy drop as she coated my face with her pleasure. I wanted to savor this moment, but I was rock hard in my slacks, ready to feel that slickness on my cock.

The moment calmed and she let me wrap my arms around her as she spasmed and whimpered coming down from the high of her orgasm.

I moved a tendril of hair behind her ear and kissed her brow. "You did so well for me, Little Elf."

After a few long minutes she wiggled closer

into my body, "I'm sorry about the mess."

"I fucking love the mess."

"But what if it stains?" She twisted in my arms so we were face to face.

"I'll clean it."

"What if it doesn't come clean? This looks like an expensive couch..." she worried her lower lip.

I pulled her lip away from her gnawing and kissed her. She eagerly met my tongue with hers, and we laid there, making out like teenagers on my couch.

When we separated, her breaths were shallow and mine were stuck in my throat somewhere.

"I'll get a new one." I told her, I didn't give a shit about the couch. It was just a thing, *her*, on the other hand, she was irreplaceable.

She rolled her eyes and sat up, stretching

her arms over her head and giving me the best fucking view a man could ask for. The way her breasts curved roundly into a handle of skin that I wanted to explore every inch of... I was sure I had drooled all over myself watching her stand on shaky legs and walk into the bathroom.

Her juicy ass bounced and swayed, and those damn stockings had me almost begging her to let me fuck her like a raging asshole.

But I wouldn't.

Because the moment I get to slide my cock between her legs I was going to savor every fucking minute.

Ash

Joy t His Dick

**"Joy to his dick, the orgasm has come
Let me receive his cum."**

I was so gone. Way further than I thought I would be. I didn't want to be addicted, but fuck he was a beautiful man with a filthy mouth, and if he could make me feel that good with just his mouth and fingers, God only knew what he could do with his cock.

I cleaned myself up in his bathroom, fluffing my hair and putting my thong back on. It should have felt weird, prancing around in just stockings and barely any underwear, but the way his eyes heated every time he saw me was like licks of flames on my body.

Like a drug, filling me with the most exquisite feeling alive.

His footsteps lingered near the doorway, as if he too didn't want to be separated for too long.

I laughed and opened the door, "Missing me already?"

His hands immediately went to my hips and he pulled me flush against him.

"I can't explain it." He buried his face in my neck, causing me to shiver, and when he took a deep breath and sighed... well, I'm glad he was holding me up, because my knees forgot how to work.

I nodded, because I understood what he meant. I couldn't rationalize my reaction to him, the deep set knowing. It just felt right to be here, enjoying each other's bodies.

"Can I get you some water?" He asked, eyes

tracing my face.

"Got anything with some bubbles?"

He laughed, "I do, actually."

Grabbing my hand, he led me out of the bathroom. Into the small, but tidy, kitchen. It had a few cabinets resting above the counter, and a row below. I hopped up onto the granite and swayed my legs.

He eyed me, and I smirked, "I'm a furniture sitter."

His laugh was husky and deep, just what I imagined it would be from our many emails back and forth. There was a time that I thought he had no sense of humor at all, that he was just a stick in the mud with no personality to spare.

Then one day I found it. He had a very dry sense of humor, almost undetectable in written correspondence, but it was there and I knew then that we would be alright.

What I didn't see coming was this. Being half naked in my boss's apartment, with two orgasms *he* gave me under my belt, with him cracking me open a bottle of Cheerwine.

"My mother always told me not to take drinks from strangers," I said, giving him a wink and taking a long sip of the cool soda. It was exactly what I needed.

"I'd hardly call us strangers."

His cheeky little smile made me lean back and laugh. "New achievement unlocked. Strangers with benefits."

"You're so weird," he said, spreading my thighs on the cold surface and standing between them. "But, I really like it."

I leaned into him, wrapping my arms around his shoulders and connecting our foreheads. It was nice, just existing with him. He ran his hands up my back, kneading and massaging in slow circles.

The feeling gave me all the sugar plum fairies fluttering around in my stomach.

After a moment, he leaned back, "Done with your bubbles?"

"I only had one sip!" I protested, the cherry fizzy liquid was so good, I took another gulp.

He lifted a brow and began rolling down my Christmas stockings, one leg at a time. He tantalizingly rolled them down my calves and threw them over his shoulder.

His lips met mine in a gentle caress, while his tongue ran the seam of my lips, a question without the words.

I opened, mingling my tongue with his, as I worked the buttons free on his dress shirt. Running my hands over his sculpted shoulders I pushed the material away, and he let it fall to the floor.

Holy stars.

He was packed with lean muscle, his chest was defined, and a divot ran down the middle of his stomach, to a happy trail of light hair, before meeting his hips where his flesh tapered in.

"Cheese and crackers." I sighed.

He laughed and grabbed my ass, pulling me into him. Our skin felt like it sizzled where we touched. Like magnets connecting for the first time.

"I think you're perfect too," he said, still chuckling.

I ran my hands down his sides, noting the firmness of his body. He allowed me to slip my right hand into his pants and grip his length.

He was heavy and warm while I stroked him, ready to make good on his promises.

"I need you," I said into his skin where his

shoulder met his neck.

"So impatient," he hummed authoritatively in my hair.

I nodded, because hot damn, I couldn't wait. I needed his perfect fucking cock inside of me. And I needed it now.

I was slick and aching for him to slide between my thighs.

He lifted me off the counter and sat me on my feet, "Let me watch you walk to my bed, Little Elf."

I winked and did as he instructed. "First door on the right," he said, and slapped my ass.

Twisting the handle, I opened the door. It was dark, but he flipped a switch and soft amber light illuminated his messy bed.

I didn't care, we were going to make a mess of it anyway. "Lay down for me."

I did, backing up to the head board where I

settled my head between his pillows. His spicy scent invaded my nostrils and I took a deep breath.

His hands landed on my feet, and I opened my eyes. His heated gaze was on mine, igniting an inferno of feelings in my body. He ran his hands over my ankles, calves, knees, thighs, trailing kisses behind his hands, alternating legs.

"I'm going to fuck you senseless, baby. I want my bed soaked in your cum, then I want you to say 'thank you, Boss' when I'm done with you."

I nodded, because fuck, what else could I do. His words made mine disappear.

He kissed his way up my body, paying special attention to my breasts. Sucking the hard nipples into his mouth and gently nipping at them.

His lips finally met mine in a frenzied kiss.

"Turn over onto your stomach and lift your ass," he whispered while sitting up to shift onto his knees, "Then spread your fucking pussy open for me like the good little whore you are."

Fucking *stars*, I swear his words would be the death of me, but I did as he asked, leaning on my shoulder and reaching under my stomach to get between my legs. I used my fingers to pull myself apart, and exposed myself to him fully.

He groaned, "Fucking hell," before plunging into my pussy, bare and setting an unrelenting pace. His palm cracked across my ass as he worked me into a blissful frenzy.

Just when I felt my orgasm beginning he pulled out and I whimpered at the loss.

"Boss," I whined.

"Yes, Little Elf?"

"I was *right* there," I complained.

"I know," he said wickedly. I could see him

stroking his cock from over my shoulder, and I loved how his hand just barely wrapped around it. He squeezed and rubbed his tip over my dripping entrance. "How badly do you want to cum, my perfect plaything?"

"So, so badly." I managed to whimper out, moving my fingers toward my clit.

The back of his hand clipped my ass as he swatted my hands away, "Mine," he growled.

"Please, Boss. God, *please*, I need it."

"I love the way you beg for my cock," he grumbled and leisurely slid back into my aching cunt.

He moved inside of me, torturously slow as my pleasure rose higher and higher. My pussy tightened as he thrust into me, over and over driving me so far into bliss I couldn't see straight.

When I felt my orgasm start to spiral into a

white hot sensation he pulled out, shoved two fingers inside of me, massaging the spot that had me crying into the sheets. He rubbed the tip of his cock against my clit as I soaked his hips.

Cum cascaded out of my body as he worked me over with expert precision. He removed his fingers, and shoved his cock so far into my tightening pussy his hips smacked my ass. I made a noise I wasn't sure I had ever made before, like a moan-scream. It was visceral, and raw, and I wanted him to make me do it again.

My vision blacked out and my muscles locked down as pleasure wracked my body, and I made the biggest fucking mess of my life on him and his sheets.

"That's my good fucking Elf," he growled in my ear, "Soaking my cock with your cum."

I couldn't speak, words escaped my blissfully

spent mind.

"Don't worry, baby," he crooned, "I'm not done yet."

He flipped my pliable body over, and kissed me. Hooking my knees over his elbows he pushed his cock all the way back inside of my drenched pussy. My back arched, I couldn't go again.

"One more," he said, as if reading my mind.

His movements were short and harsh, hips smacking into mine. The sound was erotic, and quite possibly my new favorite sound.

His breaths were labored and it was so fucking sexy to see him so untethered. So disheveled with bringing me pleasure.

I wrapped one hand around the back of his neck and gently pulled him to me. Our lips brushed as I began to speak.

"Cum with me," I breathed against his mouth.

His eyes fluttered shut and he rumbled deep in his chest, "Fuck, Ash."

I moaned as he surrendered one of my legs and wrapped his hand around my neck to kiss me breathless. Fire erupted low in my belly as I felt his cock twitch inside of me.

"I'm there," I whined, "please, Boss."

I felt his smile as he nibbled my neck, "You want me to fill your tight wet pussy with my cum?"

"Yes!" I screamed.

He pounded into me and an orgasm that I hadn't known was building inside of me rocked me to my fucking soul. My legs straightened out as my arms tightened, clutching him tighter to me, my pussy contracting around him.

He lost it.

His moan was so deep and growly that I could *feel* the rumble everywhere as he released deep inside of me. His cock throbbed as he poured hot cum inside of me. When he finally pulled out and rested his weight on top of me I felt so full, and sated, and *happy*. It was delicious and I couldn't help the aftershocks of rapture that twitched in my muscles.

We laid there, breaths heavy and mingling for a few minutes, enjoying the safety of falling with each other.

He rested his lips against my neck, "That was..."

"I know," I giggled, delirious.

Monday came around way too damn fast. I wasn't ready to let her go just yet, which was... odd. I couldn't remember the last time I'd wanted nothing more than to *keep* someone in my orbit.

These past two days were the best of my life, and not just because of the sex... though that was otherworldly. She was quirky and fun, and her laugh... it was magic.

She was pulling on her green tights over those smooth golden brown legs that I had kissed, bitten, and licked.

"Stay," I blurted.

She whirled around, almost tipping over and I jumped up to steady her. Her eyes found mine, and I swear I saw something in her gaze. It felt like electricity shot through my body every time her eyes landed on mine, and I wanted this feeling to last forever.

I wasn't naive enough to think one weekend with me would make her feelings that strong, but a part of me hoped it would, that she would feel just as fiercely for me as I did for her.

Laughing, she rubbed my arms up and down, "We have to go into the office today, remember?"

Fuck.

I totally forgot about the gift exchange.

"You forgot, didn't you?" She smiled even wider and sighed dramatically like she didn't know what to do with me. "Good thing I got an extra present, huh?"

My eyes widened and my brows went sky high. "You did what?"

"I got an extra because, you aren't exactly the most cheerful man I've ever met, *Boss*. I figured you would have too much on your mind to remember the exchange. Even though Becks sets it up every year."

"But you don't know who I drew out of the pot of names," I argued.

"Have you ever heard of gift cards?"

We both laughed, and damn it, I knew, I knew I had to keep her. I had to confess how I felt, and if she didn't feel the same... well, at least I'd tried.

"Ashtrid," I began, and her eyes immediately filled with tears, "I really, really, probably way too much, enjoyed this weekend."

She nodded, "Me too."

Her words were a broken whisper, and I

wanted to comfort her. I wanted to make her feel the same way I did, like together we could be powerful and strong.

"Could I..." I began, and cleared my throat, "See you again?"

Her eyes flickered away and she bit the inside of her lip, the skin sucked in and puckered, as if she had to really think. Maybe I was the fool, maybe this was only about sex for her, and I don't know how I would feel if that's all this was.

"Of course you'll see me again," she responded, "You're my boss."

"That's not..."

She laughed and placed her palm over my heart. "Tell you what, if you come to the gift exchange, I'll give you my answer."

She pulled away and threw her dress on, over her messy hair she had thrown up into a bun.

She smoothed the skirt, grabbed her purse and walked to the door.

"I really hope I'll see you there," she said before giving me a wink and walking out.

Oh, I'd be there, and I was going to have the best gift.

Becks somehow had the converted hotel, which served as M&W Enterprises headquarters, altered into a Christmas wonderland. It was decorated even more seriously than *The Barn* where I'd seen Ash for the first time.

I walked through the lobby, smoothing my button down over my stomach nervously. I was queasy, anticipating seeing her again. She wasn't hard to find, wearing a dress made of sparkles, or sequins, or whatever they were called.

The red dress made her look like a Christmas goddess and I wasted no time crossing the room to where she stood with Becks.

"Hi," Ash said, allowing me to press a kiss against her cheek.

Becks eyed us and slowly her lips turned up into a knowing grin.

"Hello, Peacock," she said with mirth in her voice, "How was *your* weekend?"

"Knock it off, Gran," Ash said, rolling her eyes.

"You're no fun," Becks replied and patted my arm.

We watched Becks walk to another cluster of people in the room and absorb into the conversation.

When I turned fully back to Ash she handed me a small gift wrapped box, and I looked between her and the box. The silver wrapping was shiny, and perfectly done up. The ribbon was wrapped around the sides and tied into a neat little bow on top.

"Open it," Ash said, practically bouncing on her toes.

I slid my fingers under the ribbon and pulled it off. I didn't want to damage the wrapping, so I carefully pulled up the taped paper and I swear she started vibrating.

"Come on!" She said, "Rip it open already!"

I chuckled, "That *eager*, huh?"

Her cheeks tinged pink and her teeth sunk into her lower lip. "It suits me, so I've been told."

I coughed and nodded, opening the velvet box she presented me with. When the hinges

snapped open I had to turn it sideways to read
the note inside.

I'd love to go on a date.
If you still want me
say,
"Merry Christmas" boss,
and I'll know.

Eli

End Call

"And?" Ronnie all but screeched in my ear. "What happened?"

"I said 'Merry Fucking Christmas'."

I could hear her squealing on the other line with Finn in the background asking her what was wrong.

"Eli is getting married!" Ronnie shouted at him, and he chuckled while saying, "Congrats man."

"And I wanted to know if you and Bellamy would plan it?" I asked, "Before I tell Ash I knew you."

"Of course we will! Do you have a date? It's

not like in two weeks, right?"

"Slow down," I laughed, "I don't know when, I just know I want whatever she wants."

"Eli! I'm so happy for you!"

"Appy!" I heard a little voice in the background.

"Yes Atlas! Happy!" She clapped, and must have picked him up because his little excited noises got louder. "Email me her contact, we'll get y'all squared away!"

"Thank you, Ronnie." I really meant it, I was head over heels for this woman, and I wanted her to have the best experience.

"I'm glad you're happy, Eli. You're such a good man, and I can't wait to meet the woman who finally locked you down," she said, her voice softer now.

"Me too." I knew I had a stupid cheesy grin on my face, but I didn't care. My girl was going to have the wedding of her dreams, and it's all because I fake dated my brother's wedding planner a few years ago.

I couldn't wait to tell Ash, she was going to lose her mind, and then I'd fuck her senseless after.

Acknowledgments

When I couldn't stop thinking about Eli after Firecracker, I knew he wouldn't stop yelling in my head until had his own happy ending. Emphasis on *happy*. So when I started to write this smutty little novella I knew I had to rope in my editor. Trinity, you made this passion project a smutty **good** time. I also love all of your reactions, I wouldn't be able to write without them. Seriously, I think I may have a problem...or complex. I know I probably give you a mild heart attack every time I send you out-of-the-blue messages like..."I did a thing." So thank you for being an amazing friend, and editor, who is always on board for my wild ideas.

To the two Ashley's in my life, thank you both for being so loving and passionate about all of my projects. Both of you are integral to my writing, and I love the absolute feral energy you both give me.

To my illustrator, Roze, you are always there when I contact you for a commission, and I will forever be grateful for all the hard work you do for me! If my readers are ever looking for an illustrator who is kind and patient, I will send them your way every time. You are an amazing artist, and I adore your work!

Finally, because I always save the best for last, to everyone who has picked up Boss, or Firecracker, thank you. I wouldn't be where I am, or be able to create these stories, without y'all.

Words can't express how much I enjoyed writing this one, and I hope you had just as much fun reading it.

About the Author

Taylor Wilson-West is a firm believer that the magic of words on a page can transport readers to new places, and finds comfort in making new, albeit fictional, friends. Currently residing in a small town in North Carolina with her husband and two perfect kiddos, she lives off Cheerwine, potatoes, and ranch dressing. When she's not reading or writing, she can be found shopping at bookstores, adding to her never ending bookshelves. Taylor finds it necessary to have a bookish candle that fits every genre and book character that she has ever fallen in love with. Her favorite moment in any consumable media is when confident, fat main characters get their happily ever after.

If you've made it this far, please leave a review! Reviews are an author's best friend, and readers obviously! :P

GoodReads

Amazon

Find me here:

Instagram